D1362885

HORRiD
HENRY
AND THE
FOOTBALL FiEND

Francesca Simon spent her childhood on the
beach in California, and then went to Yale and
Oxford Universities to study medieval history
and literature. She now lives in London with
her English husband and their son. When she
is not writing books she is doing theatre and
restaurant reviews or chasing after her Tibetan
Spaniel, Shanti.

Books by Francesca Simon

Don't Cook Cinderella
Helping Hercules

and for younger readers

Don't Be Horrid, Henry
Illustrated by Kevin McAleenan

The Topsy-Turvies
Illustrated by Emily Bolam

There is a complete list of Horrid Henry
titles at the end of the book.

HORRID HENRY

AND THE

FOOTBALL FIEND

Francesca Simon
Illustrated by Tony Ross

Orion
Children's Books

First published in Great Britain in 2006
by Orion Children's Books
a division of the Orion Publishing Group Ltd
Orion House
5 Upper St Martin's Lane
London WC2H 9EA
An Hachette Livre UK Company

10

Text © Francesca Simon 2006
Illustrations © Tony Ross 2006

The moral right of Francesca Simon and Tony Ross
to be identified as author and illustrator of this
work has been asserted.

A catalogue record for this book is
available from the British Library.

Printed in Great Britain by
Clays Ltd, St Ives plc

www.orionbooks.co.uk

To Elaine and Mark Eisenthal,
and to Alexander, Josh and Katherine

CONTENTS

1

HORRID HENRY PEEKS AT PETER'S DIARY

'What are you doing?' demanded Horrid Henry, bursting into Peter's bedroom.

'Nothing,' said Perfect Peter quickly, slamming his notebook shut.

'Yes you are,' said Henry.

'Get out of my room,' said Peter. 'You're not allowed to come in unless I say so.'

Horrid Henry leaned over Peter's shoulder.

'What are you writing?'

'None of your business,' said Peter. He

1

covered the closed notebook tightly
with his arm.

'It is *too* my business if you're writing
about *me*.'

'It's *my* diary. I can write what I want
to,' said Peter. 'Miss Lovely said we
should keep a diary for a week and
write in it every day.'

'Bo-ring,' said Henry, yawning.

'No it isn't,' said Peter. 'Anyway, you'll
find out next week what I'm writing:
I've been chosen to read my diary out
loud for our class assembly.'

Horrid Henry's heart turned to ice.

Peter read his diary out loud? So the
whole school could hear Peter's lies
about him? No way!

'Gimme that!' screamed Horrid Henry,
lunging for the diary.

'No!' screamed Peter, holding on tight.
'MUUUM! Help! Henry's in my room!

2

And he didn't knock! And he won't leave!'

'Shut up, tattle-tale,' hissed Henry, forcing Peter's fingers off the diary.

'MUUUUMMMMMM!' shrieked Peter.

Mum stomped up the stairs.

Henry opened the diary. But before he could read a single word Mum burst in.

'He snatched my diary! And he told me to shut up!' wailed Peter.

'Henry! Stop annoying your brother,' said Mum.

'I wasn't,' said Henry.

'Yes he was,' snivelled Peter.

'And now you've made him cry,' said Mum. 'Say sorry.'

'I was just asking about his homework,' protested Henry innocently.

'He was trying to read my diary,' said Peter.

'Henry!' said Mum. 'Don't be horrid. A diary is private. Now leave your brother alone.'

It was so unfair. Why did Mum always believe Peter?

Humph. Horrid Henry stalked out of Peter's bedroom. Well, no way was Henry waiting until class assembly to find out what Peter had written.

Sneak. Sneak. Sneak.

Horrid Henry checked to the right. Horrid Henry checked to the left. Mum was downstairs working on the computer.

4

Dad was in the garden. Peter was playing at Goody-Goody Gordon's house.

At last, the coast was clear. He'd been trying to get hold of Peter's diary for days. There was no time to lose.

Tomorrow was Peter's class assembly. Would he mention Sunday's food fight, when Henry had been forced to throw soggy pasta at Peter? Or when Henry had to push Peter off the comfy black chair and pinch him? Or yesterday when Henry banished him from the

Purple Hand Club and Peter had run scream-ing to Mum?

A lying, slimy worm like Peter would be sure to make it look like Henry was the villain when in fact Peter was always to blame.

Even worse, what horrid lies had Peter been making up about him? People would read Peter's ravings and think they were true. When Henry was famous, books would be written about him, and someone would find Peter's diary and believe it! When things were written down they had a horrible way of seeming to be true even when they were big fat lies.

Henry sneaked into Peter's bedroom

and shut the door. Now, where was that
diary? Henry glanced at Peter's tidy
desk. Peter kept it on the second shelf,
next to his crayons and trophies.

The diary was gone.

Rats. Peter must have hidden it.

That little worm, thought Horrid
Henry. Why on earth would he hide his
diary? And *where* on earth would that
smelly toad hide it? Behind his 'Good as
Gold' certificates? In the laundry basket?
Underneath his stamp collection?

He checked Peter's sock drawer. No
diary.

He checked Peter's underwear drawer. No diary.

He peeked under Peter's pillow, and under Peter's bed.

Still no diary.

OK, where would *I* hide a diary, thought Horrid Henry desperately. Easy. I'd put it in a chest and bury it in the garden, with a pirate curse on it.

Somehow he doubted Perfect Peter would be so clever.

OK, thought Henry, if I were an ugly toad like him, where would I hide it?

The bookcase. Of course. What better place to hide a book?

Henry strolled over to Peter's bookcase, with all the books arranged neatly in alphabetical order. Aha! What

8

was that sticking out between *The Happy Nappy* and *The Hoppy Hippo*?

Gotcha, thought Horrid Henry, yanking the diary off the shelf. At last he would know Peter's secrets. He'd make him cross out all his lies if it was the last thing he did.

Horrid Henry sat down and began to read:

<u>Monday</u>
Today I drew a picture of my teacher,
Miss Lovely. Miss Lovely gave me a
gold star for reading. That's because
I'm the best reader in the class. And
the best at maths. And the best at
everything else.

<u>Tuesday</u>
Today I said please and thank you
236 times

<u>Wednesday</u>
Today I ate all my vegetables

Thursday
Today I sharpened my pencils.
I ate all my sprouts and had
seconds.

Friday
Today I wrote a poem to my mummy
    I Love my mummy,
    I came out of her tummy,
    Her food is yummy,
    She is so scrummy,
    I love my mummy.

Slowly Horrid Henry closed Peter's
diary. He knew Peter's diary would be
bad. But never in his worst nightmares
had he imagined anything this bad.

Perfect Peter hadn't mentioned him
once. Not once.

You'd think I didn't even live in this
house, thought Henry. He was outraged.

11

How dare Peter *not* write about him?
And then all the stupid things Peter *had*
written.

Henry's name would be mud when
people heard Peter's diary in assembly
and found out what a sad brother he
had. Everyone would tease him. Horrid
Henry would never live down the
shame.

Peter needed Henry's help, and he
needed it fast. Horrid Henry grabbed a
pencil and got to work.

<u>Monday</u>
Today I drew a picture of my teacher,
Miss Lovely. I drew her with Piggy
ears and a grate big giant belly
Then I turned it into a
dartbord Miss Lovely gave me
a gold star for reading. Miss
Lovely is my worst teecher
ever. She should reely be
called Miss Lumpy.
Miss Dumpy Lumpy is wot Gordon
and I call her behind her back.
Tee hee, she'll never know!

I'm the best reader in the class. And

the best at maths. And the best at everything else. Too bad I have smelly pants and nitty hair

That's more like it, thought Horrid Henry.

<u>Tuesday</u>
Today I said please and thank you 236 times

~~The~~ Not! I called Mum a big blobby pants face. I called Dad a stinky fish. Then I played Pirats with the worlds greatest brother, Henry. I Wish I were as clever as Henry. But I know thats imposibel.

<u>Wednesday</u>
Today I ate all my vegetables

14

Then I sneeked loads of sweets from the sweet jar and lied to dad about it. I am a very good liar. No one should ever beleeve a word I say. Henry gets the blame but reely every thing is always my fault.

Thursday

Today I sharpened my pencils. Alt the better to write rude notes!

I ate all my sprouts and had seconds. Then threw up all over Mum. Eeugh, what a smell. I reely am a smelly toad. I am so lucky to have a grate brother like Henry. He is always so nice to me Hip Hip Hurray for Henry

Friday
Today I wrote a poem to my Dummy
I Love my Dummy,
It's my best chummy
It tastes so yummy,
It is so scrummy,
I love my Dummy.

Much better, thought Horrid Henry. Now that's what I call a diary. Everyone would have died of boredom otherwise.

Henry carefully replaced Peter's diary in the bookcase. I hope Peter appreciates what I've done for him, thought Horrid Henry.

The entire school gathered in the hall for assembly. Peter's class sat proudly on benches at the front. Henry's class sat cross-legged on the floor. The parents sat on chairs down both sides.

Mum and Dad waved at Peter. He waved shyly back.

Miss Lovely stood up.

'Hello Mums and Dads, boys and girls, welcome to our class assembly. This term our class has been keeping diaries. We're going to read some of them to you now. First to read will be Peter. Everyone pay attention, and see if you too can be as good as I know Peter has been. I'd like everyone here to copy one of Peter's good deeds. I know I can't wait to hear how he has spent this last week.'

Peter stood up, and opened his diary. In a big loud voice, he read:

'MONDAY

'Today I drew a picture of my teacher, Miss Lovely.'

Peter glanced up at Miss Lovely. She beamed at him.

'I drew her with piggy ears and a great big giant belly. Then I turned it into a dartboard.'

What??! It was always difficult to read out loud and understand what he had read, but something didn't sound right. He didn't remember writing about a pig with a big belly. Nervously Peter looked up at Mum and Dad. Was he imagining it, or did their smiles seem more like

frowns? Peter shook his head, and
carried on.

'Miss Lovely gave me a gold star for
reading.'

Phew, that was better! He must have
misheard himself before.

'Miss Lovely is my worst teacher ever.
She should really be called Miss Lumpy.
Miss Dumpy Lumpy—'

'Thank you, that's quite enough,'
interrupted Miss Lovely sternly, as the
school erupted in shrieks of laughter.
Her face was pink. 'Peter,
see me after assembly.
Ted will now tell
us all about
skeletons.'

'But—but—'
gasped Perfect
Peter. 'I—I didn't,
I never—'

'Sit down and be quiet,' said the head, Mrs Oddbod. 'I'll see you *and* your parents later.'

'WAAAAAAAAAA!' wailed Peter.

Mum and Dad stared at their feet. Why had they ever had children? Where was a trapdoor when you needed one?

'Waaaaaaaa,' whimpered Mum and Dad.

Naturally, Henry got into trouble. Big big trouble. It was so unfair. Why didn't anyone believe him when he said he'd improved Peter's diary for his own good? Honestly, he would never *ever* do Peter a favour again.

2

....

HORRiD HENRY AND THE FOOTBALL FiEND

'. . . AND with 15 seconds to go it's Hot-Foot Henry racing across the pitch! Rooney tries a slide tackle but Henry's too quick! Just look at that step-over! Oh no, he can't score from that distance, it's crazy, it's impossible, oh my goodness, he cornered the ball, it's IN!!!! It's IN! Another *spectacular* goal! Another spectacular win! And it's all thanks to Hot-Foot Henry, the greatest footballer who's ever lived!'

'Goal! Goal! Goal!' roared the crowd. Hot-Foot Henry had won the match! His teammates carried him through the fans, cheering and chanting, 'Hen-ry! Hen-ry! Hen-ry!'

'HENRY!'

Horrid Henry looked up to see Miss Battle-Axe leaning over his table and glaring at him with her red eyes.

'What did I just say?'

'Henry,' said Horrid Henry.

Miss Battle-Axe scowled.

'I'm watching you, Henry,' she snapped. 'Now class, please pay attention, we need to discuss—'

'Waaaaa!' wailed Weepy William.

'Susan, stop pulling my hair!' squealed Vain Violet.

24

'Miss!' shouted Inky Ian, 'Ralph's snatched my pen!'

'Didn't!' shouted Rude Ralph.

'Did!' shouted Inky Ian.

'Class! Be quiet!' bellowed Miss Battle-Axe.

'Waaaaa!' wailed Weepy William.

'Owwww!' squealed Vain Violet.

'Give it back!' shouted Inky Ian.

'Fine,' said Miss Battle-Axe, 'we won't talk about football.'

William stopped wailing.

Violet stopped squealing.

Ian stopped shouting.

Henry stopped daydreaming.

Everyone in the class stared at Miss Battle-Axe. Miss Battle-Axe wanted to talk about . . . football? Was this an alien Miss Battle-Axe?

'As you all know, our local team, Ashton Athletic, has reached the sixth round of the FA Cup,' said Miss Battle-Axe.

'YEY!' shrieked the class.

'And I'm sure you all know what happened last night . . .'

Last night! Henry could still hear the announcer's glorious words as he and Peter had gathered round the radio as the draw for round six was announced.

'Number 16, Ashton Athletic, will be playing . . .' there was a long pause as the announcer drew another ball from the hat . . . 'number 7, Manchester United.'

'Go Ashton!' shrieked Horrid Henry.

'As I was saying, before I was so rudely interrupted—' Miss Battle-Axe glared at Horrid Henry, 'Ashton are playing Manchester United in a few weeks. Every local primary school has been given a pair of tickets. And thanks to my good luck in the teacher's draw, the lucky winner will come from our class.'

'Me!' screamed Horrid Henry.

'Me!' screamed Moody Margaret.

'Me!' screamed Tough Toby, Aerobic

Al, Fiery Fiona and Brainy Brian.

'No one who shouts out will be getting anything,' said Miss Battle-Axe. 'Our class will be playing a football match at lunchtime. The player of the match will win the tickets. I'm the referee and my decision will be final.'

Horrid Henry was so stunned that for a moment he could scarcely breathe. FA Cup tickets! FA Cup tickets to see his local team Ashton play against Man U! Those tickets were like gold dust. Henry had begged and pleaded with Mum and Dad to get tickets, but naturally they were all sold out by the time Henry's mean, horrible, lazy parents managed to heave their stupid bones to the phone. And now here was another chance to go to the match of the century!

Ashton Athletic had never got so far in the Cup. Sure, they'd knocked out the Tooting Tigers (chant: Toot Toot! Grrr!) the Pynchley Pythons and the Cheam Champions but—Manchester United! Henry had to go to the game. He just had to. And all he had to do was be man of the match.

There was just one problem. Unfortunately, the best footballer in the class wasn't Horrid Henry. Or Aerobic Al. Or Beefy Bert.

The best footballer in the class was Moody Margaret. The second best player in the class was Moody Margaret. The third best player in the class was

Moody Margaret. It was so unfair! Why should Margaret of all people be so fantastic at football?

Horrid Henry was brilliant at shirt pulling. Horrid Henry was superb at

screaming 'Offside!' (whatever that
meant). No one could howl 'Come on,
ref!' louder. And at toe-treading,
elbowing, barging, pushing, shoving and
tripping, Horrid Henry had no equal.
The only thing Horrid Henry wasn't
good at was playing football.

But never mind. Today would be
different. Today he would dig deep
inside and find the power to be Hot-
Foot Henry—for real. Today no one
would stop him. FA Cup match here I
come, thought Horrid Henry gleefully.

Lunchtime!

Horrid Henry's class dashed to the
back playground, where the pitch was
set up. Two jumpers either end marked
the goals. A few parents gathered on the
sidelines.

Miss Battle-Axe split the class into

two teams: Aerobic Al was captain of Henry's team, Moody Margaret was captain of the other.

There she stood in midfield, having nabbed a striker position, smirking confidently. Horrid Henry glared at her from the depths of the outfield.

'Na na ne nah nah, I'm sure to be man of the match,' trilled Moody Margaret, sticking out her tongue at him. 'And you-ooo won't.'

'Shut up, Margaret,' said Henry. When he was king, anyone named Margaret would be boiled in oil and fed to the crows.

'Will you take me to the match, Margaret?' said Susan. 'After all, *I'm* your best friend.'

Moody Margaret scowled. 'Since when?'

'Since always!' wailed Susan.

'Huh!' said Margaret. 'We'll just have to see how nice you are to me, won't we?'

'Take me,' begged Brainy Brian. 'Remember how I helped you with those fractions?'

'And called me stupid,' said Margaret.

'Didn't,' said Brian.

'Did,' said Margaret.

Horrid Henry eyed his classmates.

33

Everyone looking straight ahead, everyone determined to be man of the match. Well, wouldn't they be in for a shock when Horrid Henry waltzed off with those tickets!

'Go Margaret!' screeched Moody Margaret's mum.

'Go Al!' screeched Aerobic Al's dad.

'Everyone ready?' said Miss Battle-Axe. 'Bert! Which team are you on?'

'I dunno,' said Beefy Bert.

Miss Battle-Axe blew her whistle.

Kick-off!

Kick.

 **Chase.**

Kick.

Dribble.

Dribble.

Pass.

Kick.

Save!

Goal Kick

Henry stood disconsolately on the left wing, running back and forth as the play passed him by. How could he ever be man of the match stuck out here? Well, no way was he staying in this stupid spot a moment longer.

Horrid Henry abandoned his position and chased after the ball. All the other defenders followed him.

Moody Margaret had the ball. Horrid Henry ran up behind her. He glanced at Miss Battle-Axe. She was busy chatting to Mrs Oddbod. Horrid Henry went for a two foot slide tackle and tripped her.

'Foul!' screeched Margaret. 'He hacked my leg!'

'Liar!' screeched Henry. 'I just went for the ball!'

'Cheater!' screamed Moody Margaret's mum.

'Play on,' ordered Miss Battle-Axe.

38

Yes! thought Horrid Henry triumphantly. After all, what did blind old Miss Battle-Axe know about the rules of football? Nothing. This was his golden chance to score.

Now Jazzy Jim had the ball.

Horrid Henry trod on his toes, elbowed him, and grabbed the ball.

'Hey, we're on the same team!' yelped Jim.

Horrid Henry kept dribbling.

'Pass! Pass!' screamed Al. 'Man on!'

Henry ignored him. Pass the ball? Was Al mad? For once Henry had the ball and he was keeping it.

Then suddenly Moody Margaret
appeared from behind, barged him,
dribbled the ball past Henry's team and
kicked it straight past Weepy William
into goal. Moody Margaret's team
cheered.

Weepy William burst into tears.

'Waaaaaa,' wailed Weepy William.

'Idiot!' screamed Aerobic Al's dad.

'She cheated!' shrieked Henry. 'She
fouled me!'

'Didn't,' said Margaret.

'How dare you call my daughter a
cheater?' screamed
Margaret's mum.

Miss Battle-
Axe blew her
whistle.

'Goal to
Margaret's team. The
score is one-nil.'

41

Horrid Henry gritted his teeth. He would score a goal if he had to trample on every player to do so.

Unfortunately, everyone else seemed to have the same idea.

'Ralph pushed me!' shrieked Aerobic Al.

'Didn't!' lied Rude Ralph. 'It was just a barge.'

'He used his hands, I saw him!' howled Al's father. 'Send him off.'

'I'll send *you* off if you don't behave,' snapped Miss Battle-Axe, looking up and blowing her whistle.

'It was kept in!' protested Henry.

'No way!' shouted Margaret. 'It went past the line!'

'That was ball to hand!' yelled Kind Kasim.

'No way!' screamed Aerobic Al. 'I just went for the ball.'

'Liar!'

'Liar!'

'Free kick to Margaret's team,' said Miss Battle-Axe.

'Ouch!' screamed Soraya, as Brian stepped on her toes, grabbed the ball, and headed it into goal past Kasim.

'Hurray!' cheered Al's team.

'Foul!' screamed Margaret's team.

'Score is one all,' said Miss Battle-Axe. 'Five more minutes to go.'

AAARRRGGHH! thought Horrid Henry. I've got to score a goal to have a chance to be man of the match. I've just got to. But how, how?

Henry glanced at Miss Battle-Axe. She appeared to be rummaging in her handbag. Henry saw his chance. He stuck out his foot as Margaret hurtled past.

Crash!

Margaret tumbled.

Henry seized the ball.

'Henry hacked my leg!' shrieked Margaret.

'Did not!' shrieked Henry. 'I just went for the ball.'

'REF!' screamed Margaret.

'He cheated!' screamed Margaret's mum. 'Are you blind, ref?'

Miss Battle-Axe glared.

'My eyesight is perfect, thank you,' she snapped.

Tee hee, chortled Horrid Henry.

Henry trod on Brian's toes, elbowed him, then grabbed the ball. Then Dave elbowed Henry, Ralph trod on Dave's toes, and Susan seized the ball and kicked it high overhead.

Henry looked up. The ball was high, high up. He'd never reach it, not unless, unless— Henry glanced at Miss Battle-Axe. She was watching a traffic warden patrolling outside the school gate. Henry leapt into the air and whacked the ball with his hand.

Thwack!

The ball hurled across the goal.

'Goal!' screamed Henry.

'He used his hands!' protested Margaret.

'No way!' shouted Henry. 'It was the hand of God!'

'Hen-ry! Hen-ry! Hen-ry!' cheered his team.

'Unfair!' howled Margaret's team.

Miss Battle-Axe blew her whistle.

'Time!' she bellowed. 'Al's team wins 2-1.'

'Yes!' shrieked Horrid Henry, punching the air. He'd scored the winning goal! He'd be man of the

47

match! Ashton Athletic versus Man U here I come!

Horrid Henry's class limped through the door and sat down. Horrid Henry sat at the front, beaming. Miss Battle-Axe had to award him the tickets after his brilliant performance and spectacular, game-winning goal. The question was, who *deserved* to be his guest?

No one.

I know, thought Horrid Henry, I'll sell my other ticket. Bet I get a million pounds for it. No, a billion pounds. Then I'll buy my own team, and play striker any time I want to. Horrid Henry smiled happily.

Miss Battle-Axe glared at her class.

'That was absolutely disgraceful,' she said. 'Cheating! Moving the goals! Shirt tugging!' she glared at Graham. 'Barging!

She glowered at Ralph. 'Pushing and shoving! Bad sportsmanship!' Her eyes swept over the class.

Horrid Henry sank lower in his seat. Oops.

'And don't get me started about offside,' she snapped.

Horrid Henry sank even lower.

'There was only one person who deserves to be player of the match,' she continued. 'One person who observed the rules of the beautiful game. One person who has nothing to be ashamed of today.'

Horrid Henry's heart leapt. *He* certainly had nothing to be ashamed of.

'. . . One person who can truly be proud of their performance . . .'

Horrid Henry beamed with pride.

'And that person is—'

'Me! screamed Moody Margaret.

'Me!' screamed Aerobic Al.

'Me! screamed Horrid Henry.

'—the referee,' said Miss Battle-Axe.

What?

Miss Battle-Axe . . . man of the match?

Miss Battle-Axe . . . a football fiend?

'IT'S NOT FAIR!' screamed the class.

'IT'S NOT FAIR!' screamed Horrid Henry.

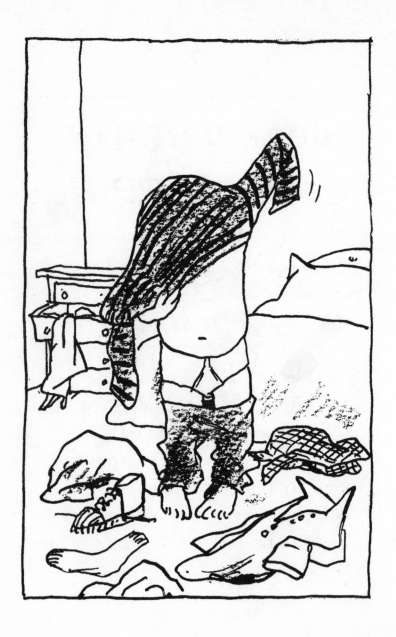

3

HORRID HENRY GOES SHOPPING

Horrid Henry stood in his bedroom up to his knees in clothes. The long sleeve stripy T-shirt came to his elbow. His trousers stopped halfway down his legs. Henry sucked in his tummy as hard as he could. Still the zip wouldn't zip.

'Nothing fits!' he screamed, yanking off the shirt and hurling it across the room. 'And my shoes hurt.'

'All right Henry, calm down,' said Mum. 'You've grown. We'll go out this afternoon and get you some new clothes and shoes.'

53

'NOOOOOOO!' shrieked Henry.
'NOOOOOOOOOOOOO!'

Horrid Henry hated shopping.

Correction: Horrid Henry loved
shopping. He loved shopping for
gigantic TVs, computer games, comics,
toys, and sweets. Yet for some reason
Horrid Henry's parents never wanted to
go shopping for good stuff. Oh no. They
shopped for hoover bags. Toothpaste.
Spinach. Socks. Why oh why did he
have such horrible parents? When he
was grown-up he'd never set foot in a

supermarket. He'd only shop for TVs,
computer games, and chocolate.

But shopping for clothes was even
worse than heaving his heavy bones
round the Happy Shopper Supermarket.
Nothing was more boring than being
dragged round miles and miles and
miles of shops, filled with disgusting
clothes only a mutant would ever want
to wear, and then standing in a little
room while Mum made you try on icky
scratchy things you wouldn't be seen
dead in if they were the last trousers on
earth. It was horrible enough getting
dressed once a day without doing it fifty
times. Just thinking about trying on shirt
after shirt after shirt made Horrid
Henry want to scream.

'I'm not going shopping!' he howled,
kicking the pile of clothes as viciously as
he could. 'And you can't make me.'

'What's all this yelling?' demanded
Dad.

'Henry needs new trousers,' said Mum
grimly.

Dad went pale.

'Are you sure?'

'Yes,' said Mum. 'Take a look at him.'

Dad looked at Henry. Henry scowled.

'They're a *little* small, but not *that* bad,'
said Dad.

'I can't breathe in these trousers!'
shrieked Henry.

'That's why we're going shopping,' said Mum. 'And *I'll* take him.' Last time Dad had taken Henry shopping for socks and came back instead with three Hairy Hellhound CDs and a jumbo pack of Day-Glo slime.

'I don't know what came over me,' Dad had said, when Mum told him off.

'But why do *I* have to go?' said Henry. 'I don't want to waste my precious time shopping.'

'What about *my* precious time?' said Mum.

Henry scowled. Parents didn't have precious time. They were there to serve their children. New trousers should just magically appear, like clean clothes and packed lunches.

Mum's face brightened. 'Wait, I have an idea,' she beamed. She rushed out and came back with a large plastic bag.

'Here,' she said, pulling out
a pair of bright red
trousers, 'try these on.'

Henry looked at them
suspiciously.

'Where are they
from?'

'Aunt Ruby dropped
off some of Steve's old
clothes a few weeks ago. I'm
sure we'll find something that fits you.'

Horrid Henry stared at Mum. Had
she gone gaga? Was she actually
suggesting that he should wear his
horrible cousin's mouldy old shirts and
pongy pants? Just imagine, putting his
arms into the same stinky sleeves that
Stuck-up Steve had slimed? Uggh!

'NO WAY!' screamed Henry,
shuddering. 'I'm not wearing Steve's
smelly old clothes. I'd catch rabies.'

'They're practically brand new,' said Mum.

'I don't care,' said Henry.

'But Henry,' said Perfect Peter. 'I always wear *your* hand-me-downs.'

'So?' snarled Henry.

'I don't mind wearing hand-me-downs,' said Perfect Peter. 'It saves so much money. You shouldn't be so selfish, Henry.'

'Quite right, Peter,' said Mum, smiling. 'At least *one* of my sons thinks about others.'

Horrid Henry pounced. He was a vampire sampling his supper.

'AAIIIEEEEEE!' squealed Peter.

'Stop that, Henry!' screamed Mum.

'Leave your brother alone!' screamed Dad.

59

Horrid Henry glared at Peter.

'Peter is a worm, Peter is a toad,' jeered Henry.

'Mum!' wailed Peter. 'Henry said I was a worm. And a toad.'

'Don't be horrid, Henry,' said Dad. 'Or no TV for a week. You have three choices. Wear Steve's old clothes. Wear your old clothes. Go shopping for new ones today.'

'Do we *have* to go today?' moaned Henry.

'Fine,' said Mum. 'We'll go tomorrow.'

'I don't want to go tomorrow,' wailed Henry. 'My weekend will be ruined.'

Mum glared at Henry.

'Then we'll go right now this minute.'

'NO!' screamed Horrid Henry.

'YES!' screamed Mum.

Several hours later, Mum and Henry
walked into Mellow Mall. Mum already
looked like she'd been crossing the
Sahara desert
without water
for days. Serve
her right for
bringing me here,
thought Horrid
Henry, scowling,
as he scuffed his
feet.

'Can't we go
to Shop 'n'
Drop?' whined Henry. 'Graham says
they've got a win your weight in
chocolate competition.'

'No,' said Mum, dragging Henry into
Zippy's Department Store. 'We're here
to get you some new trousers and shoes.
Now hurry up, we don't have all day.'

Horrid Henry looked around. Wow! There was lots of great stuff on display.

'I want the Hip-Hop Robots,' said Henry.

'No,' said Mum.

'I want the new Supersoaker!' screeched Henry.

'No,' said Mum.

'I want a Creepy Crawly lunchbox!'

'NO!' said Mum, pulling him into the boys' clothing department.

What, thought Horrid Henry grimly, is the point of going shopping if you never buy anything?

'I want Root-a-Toot trainers with flashing red lights,' said Henry. He could see himself now, strolling into class, a bugle blasting and red light flashing every time his feet hit the floor. Cool! He'd love to see Miss Battle-Axe's face when he exploded into class wearing them.

'No,' said Mum, shuddering.

'Oh please,' said Henry.

'NO!' said Mum, 'we're here to buy trousers and sensible school shoes.'

'But I want Root-a-Toot trainers!' screamed Horrid Henry. 'Why can't we buy what *I* want to buy? You're the meanest mother in the world and I hate you!'

'Don't be horrid, Henry. Go and try these on,' said Mum, grabbing a selection of hideous trousers and revolting T-shirts. 'I'll keep looking.'

Horrid Henry sighed loudly and slumped towards the dressing room. No one in the world suffered as much as he did. Maybe he could hide between the clothes racks and never come out.

Then something wonderful in the toy department next door caught his eye.

Whooa! A whole row of the new megalotronic animobotic robots with 213 programmable actions. Horrid Henry dumped the clothes and ran over to have a look. Oooh, the new Intergalactic Samurai Gorillas which launched real stinkbombs! And the latest Supersoakers! And deluxe Dungeon Drink kits with a celebrity chef recipe book! To say nothing of the Mega-Whirl Goo Shooter which sprayed fluorescent goo for fifty metres in every direction. Wow!

Mum staggered into the dressing room with more clothes. 'Henry?' said Mum.

No reply.

'HENRY!' said Mum.

Still no reply.

Mum yanked open a dressing room door.

'Hen—'

'Excuse *me!*' yelped a bald man, standing in his underpants.

'Sorry,' said Mum, blushing bright pink. She dashed out of the changing room and scanned the shop floor.

Henry was gone.

Mum searched up the aisles.

No Henry.

Mum searched down the aisles.

Still no Henry.

Then Mum saw a tuft of hair sticking up behind the neon sign for Ballistic Bazooka Boomerangs. She marched over and hauled Henry away.

'I was just looking,' protested Henry.

Henry tried on one pair of trousers after another.

'No, no, no, no, no, no, no,' said Henry, kicking off the final pair. 'I hate all of them.'

'All right,' said Mum, grimly. 'We'll look somewhere else.'

Mum and Henry went to Top Trousers. They went to Cool Clothes. They went to Stomp in the Swamp. Nothing had been right.

'Too tight,' moaned Henry.

'Too itchy!'

'Too big!'

'Too small!'

'Too ugly!'

'Too red!'

'Too uncomfortable!'

'We're going to Tip-Top Togs,' said Mum wearily. 'The first thing that fits, we're buying.'

Mum staggered into the children's department and grabbed a pair of pink and green tartan trousers in Henry's size.

'Try these on,' she ordered. 'If they fit we're having them.'

Horrid Henry gazed in horror at the horrendous trousers.

'Those are girls' trousers!' he screamed.

'They are not,' said Mum.

'Are too!' shrieked Henry.

'I'm sick and tired of your excuses,

69

Henry,' said Mum. 'Put them on or no pocket money for a year. I mean it.'

Horrid Henry put on the pink and green tartan trousers, puffing out his stomach as much as possible. Not even Mum would make him buy trousers that were too tight.

Oh no. The horrible trousers had an elastic waist. They would fit a mouse as easily as an elephant.

'And lots of room to grow,' said Mum brightly. 'You can wear them for years. Perfect.'

'NOOOOOO!' howled Henry. He flung himself on the floor kicking and screaming. 'NOOOO! THEY'RE GIRLS' TROUSERS!!!'

'We're buying them,' said Mum. She gathered up the tartan trousers and stomped over to the till. She tried not to think about starting all over again trying to find a pair of shoes that Henry would wear.

A little girl in pigtails walked out of the dressing room, twirling in pink and green tartan trousers.

'I love them, Mummy!' she shrieked.
'Let's get three pairs.'

Horrid Henry stopped howling.

He looked at Mum.

Mum looked at Henry.

Then they both looked at the pink and green tartan trousers Mum was carrying.

ROOT-A-TOOT!
ROOT-A-TOOT!
ROOT-A-TOOT!
TOOT! TOOT!

An earsplitting bugle blast shook the house. Flashing red lights bounced off the walls.

'What's that noise?' said Dad, covering his ears.

'What noise?' said Mum, pretending to read.

ROOT-A-TOOT!
ROOT-A-TOOT!
ROOT-A-TOOT!
TOOT! TOOT!

Dad stared at Mum.

'You didn't,' said Dad. 'Not—Root-a-Toot trainers?'

Mum hid her face in her hands.

'I don't know what came over me,' said Mum.

4

....

HORRID HENRY'S ARCH ENEMY

'Be bop a lu la!' boomed Jazzy Jim, be-bopping round the class and bouncing to the beat.

'One day, my prince will come . . .' warbled Singing Soraya.

'Bam bam bam bam bam!' drummed Horrid Henry, crashing his books up and down on his table top.

'Class! Settle down!' shouted Miss Battle-Axe.

'Be bop a lu la!' boomed Jazzy Jim.

'One day, my prince will come . . .' warbled Singing Soraya.

'Bam bam bam bam bam!' drummed Horrid Henry.

'Jim!' barked Miss Battle-Axe. 'Stop yowling. Soraya! Stop singing. Henry! Stop banging or everyone will miss playtime.'

'Be bop—' faltered Jim.

'. . . prince will—' squeaked Soraya.

'Bam bam bam bam bam,' drummed Horrid Henry. He was Mad Moon Madison, crazy drummer for the

Mouldy Drumsticks, whipping the
shrieking crowd into a frenzy—

'HENRY!' bellowed Miss Battle-Axe.
'STOP THAT NOISE!'

What did that ungrateful fan mean,
noise? What noise? This wasn't noise,
this was great music, this was—Mad
Moon Madison looked up from his
drum kit. Whoops.

Silence.

Miss Battle-Axe glared at her class.
Oh, for the good old days, when
teachers could whack
horrible children
with rulers.

'Linda! Stop
snoring.
Graham! Stop
drooling. Bert! Where's your chair?'

'I dunno,' said Beefy Bert.

There was a new boy standing next to

Miss Battle-Axe. His brown hair was
tightly slicked back. His shoes were
polished. He carried a trumpet and a
calculator. Yuck! He looked like a
complete idiot. Horrid Henry looked
away. And then looked back. Funny,
there was something familiar about that
boy. The way he stood with his nose in
the air. The horrid little smirk on his

face. He looked like—he looked just
like—oh no, please no, it couldn't be—
Bossy Bill! Bossy Bill!!

'Class, we have a new boy,' said Miss
Battle-Axe, doing her best to twist her
thin lips into a welcoming smile. 'I need
someone to look after him and show
him around. Who would like to be Bill's
friend for the day?'

Everyone put up their hand. Everyone
but Horrid Henry. Uggh. Bossy Bill.
What kind of cruel joke was this?

Bossy Bill was the horrible, stuck-up son of Dad's boss. Horrid Henry hated Bill. Uggh! Yuck! Just thinking about Bill made Henry gag.

Henry had a suspicion he wasn't Bill's favourite person, either. The last time they'd met, Henry had tricked Bill into photocopying his bottom. Bill had got into trouble. Big, big trouble.

Miss Battle-Axe scanned the sea of waving hands.

'Me!' shouted Moody Margaret.

'Me!' shouted Kind Kasim.

'Me!' shouted Weepy William.

'There's an empty seat next to Henry,' said Miss Battle-Axe, pointing. 'Henry will look after you.'

NO, thought Henry.

'Waaaaaa,' wailed Weepy William. 'I didn't get picked.'

'Go and sit down, Bill,' continued Miss Battle-Axe. 'Class, silent reading from page 12.'

Bossy Bill walked between the tables towards Horrid Henry.

Maybe he won't recognise me, thought Henry hopefully. After all, it was a long time ago.

Suddenly Bill stopped. His face contorted with loathing.

Oops.

He recognised me, thought Horrid Henry.

Bill marched, scowling, to the seat next to Henry and sat down. His nose wrinkled as if he smelled a stinky smell.

'You say one word about what happened at my dad's office and I'll tell my dad,' hissed Bill.

'You say one word to your dad and I'll tell everyone at school you photocopied

81

your bottom,' hissed Henry.

'Then I'll tell on you!'

'I'll tell on you!'

Bill shoved Henry.

Henry shoved Bill.

'He shoved me, miss!' shouted Bossy Bill.

'He shoved me first!' shouted Horrid Henry.

'Henry!' said Miss Battle-Axe. 'I am shocked and appalled. Is this how you welcome a new boy to our class?'

It is when the boy is Bossy Bill, thought Henry grimly.

He glared at Bill.

Bill glared at Henry.

'My old school's a lot better than this dump,' hissed Bossy Bill.

'So why don't you go back there?' hissed Henry. 'No one's stopping you.'

'Maybe I will,' said Bill.

Horrid Henry's heart leapt. Was there a chance he could get Bill to leave?

'You don't want to stay here—we get four hours of homework a night,' lied Henry.

'So?' said Bill. 'My old school gave you five hours.'

'The food's horrible.'

'Big deal,' said Bill.

'And Miss Battle-Axe is the meanest teacher in the world.'

'What did you say, Henry?' demanded Miss Battle-Axe's ice cold dagger voice.

'I just told Bill you were the keenest

teacher in the world,' said Henry quickly.

'No he didn't,' said Bill. 'He said you were the meanest.'

'Keenest,' said Henry.

'Meanest,' said Bill.

Miss Battle-Axe glared at Horrid Henry.

'I'm watching you, Henry. Now get back to work.'

DING! DING! DING!

Hurray! Saved by the playtime bell.

Horrid Henry jumped from his seat. Maybe he could escape Bill if he ran out of class fast enough.

Henry pushed and shoved his way into the hall. Free! Free at last!

'Hey!' came an unwelcome voice beside him. A sweaty hand pulled on his shirt.

'The teacher said you're supposed to show me around,' said Bossy Bill.

'OK, here are the toilets,' snarled Horrid Henry, waving his hand in

the direction of the girls' loos. 'And
the photocopier's in the office,' he
added, pointing. 'Why don't you try
it out?'

Bill scowled.

'I'm going to tell my dad that you
attacked me,' said Bill. 'In fact, I'm going
to tell my dad every single bad thing
you do in school. Then he'll tell yours
and you'll get into trouble. And won't I
laugh.'

Henry's blood boiled. What had he
ever done to deserve Bossy Bill butting
into his life? A spy in his class. Could
school get any worse?

Aerobic Al jogged past.

'Henry photocopied his bottom at my
dad's office,' said Bill loudly. 'Boy, did he
get into trouble.'

AAARRRGGHHH!

'That's a lie,' said Horrid Henry hotly.

'Bill did, not me.'

'Yeah right, Henry,' said Dizzy Dave.

'Big bottom!' shrieked Moody
Margaret.

'Big big bottom!' shrieked Sour Susan.
Bill smirked.

'Bye, big bottom,' said Bill. 'Don't
forget, I'm watching you,' he hissed.

Henry sat down by himself on the
broken bench in the secret garden. He
had to get Bill out of his class. School
was horrible enough without someone

evil like Bill spying on him and
spreading foul rumours. His life would
be ruined. He had to get rid of Bill—
fast. But how?

Maybe he could get Bill to run
screaming from school and never come
back. Wow, thought Horrid Henry.
Wouldn't that be wonderful? Bye bye
Bossy Bill.

Or maybe he could get Bill to
photocopy his
bottom again.
Probably not,
thought Horrid
Henry
regretfully. Aha!
He could trick
Bill into dancing
nude on Miss
Battle-Axe's desk
singing 'I'm a busy

bumblebee—buzz buzz buzz.' That would be sure to get him expelled. The only trouble was—how?

I've got to think of something, thought Horrid Henry desperately. I've just got to.

'Henry,' said Dad the next evening, 'my boss tells me you've been picking on his son. Bill was very upset.'

'He's picking on *me*,' protested Henry.

'And that you were told off in class for shouting out.'

'No way,' lied Henry.

'And that you broke Andrew's pencil.'

'That was an accident,' said Henry.

'And that you called Margaret nitty-face.'

'I didn't,' wailed Henry. 'Bill's lying.'

'I want you to be on your best behaviour from now on,' said Dad. 'How do you think I feel hearing these reports about you from my boss? I've never been so embarrassed in my life.'

'Who cares?' screamed Horrid Henry. 'What about me?'

'Go to your room!' shouted Dad.

'FINE!' yelled Horrid Henry, slamming the door behind him as hard as he could. I'll beat you, Bill, thought Henry, if it's the last thing I do.

Horrid Henry tried teasing Bill. Horrid Henry tried pinching Bill. He tried spreading rumours about Bill. He even tried getting Bill to punch him so Bill would be suspended.

But nothing worked. Henry just got into more and more trouble.

On Monday Dad told Henry off for making rude noises in class.

On Tuesday Dad told Henry off for

talking during storytime.

On Wednesday Dad told Henry off for not handing in his homework.

On Thursday Mum and Dad yelled at Henry for chewing gum in class, passing notes to Ralph, throwing food, jiggling his desk, pulling Margaret's hair, running down the hall and kicking a football into the back playground. Then they banned him from the computer for a week. And all because of Bossy Bill.

Horrid Henry slunk into class. It was hopeless. Bill was here to stay. Horrid Henry would just have to grit his teeth and bear it.

Miss Battle-Axe started explaining electricity.

Henry looked around the classroom. Speaking of Bill, where was he?

Maybe he has rabies, thought Horrid Henry hopefully. Or fallen down the

toilet. Better still, maybe he'd been kidnapped by aliens.

Or maybe he'd been expelled. Yes! Henry could see it now. Bill on his

knees in Mrs Oddbod's office, begging to
stay. Mrs Oddbod pointing to the door:

'Out of this school, you horrible
monster! How dare you spy on Henry,
our best pupil?'

'NOOO!' Bill would wail.

'BEGONE, WRETCH!' commanded
Mrs Oddbod. And out went Bossy Bill,
snivelling, where armed
guards were waiting
to truss him up and
take him to prison.
That must be
what had happened.

Henry smiled.
Oh joyful day!
No more
Bossy Bill,
thought
Horrid
Henry

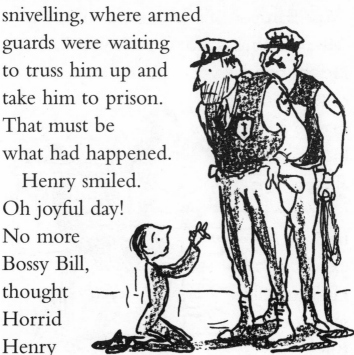

93

happily, stretching his legs under his
Bill-free table and taking a deep breath
of Bill-free air.

'Henry!' snapped Miss Battle-Axe.
'Come here.'

What now?

Slowly Horrid Henry heaved himself
out of his chair and scuffed his way to
Miss Battle-Axe's desk, where she was
busy slashing at homework with a
bright red pen.

'Bill has a sore throat,' said Miss Battle-Axe.

Rats, thought Horrid Henry. Where was the black plague when you needed it?

'His parents want him to have his homework assignments so he doesn't fall behind while he's ill,' said Miss Battle-Axe. 'If only *all* parents were so conscientious. Please give this maths worksheet to your father to give to Bill's dad.'

She handed Henry a piece of paper with ten multiplication sums on it and a large envelope.

'OK,' said Henry dully. Not even the thought of Bill lying in bed doing sums could cheer him up. All too soon Bill would be back. He was stuck with Bill for ever.

That night Horrid Henry glanced at

Bill's maths worksheet. Ten sums. Not enough, really, he thought. Why should Bill be bored in bed with nothing to do but watch TV, and read comics, and eat crisps?

And then Horrid Henry smiled. Bill wanted homework? Perhaps Henry could help. Tee hee, thought Horrid Henry, sitting down at the computer.

TAP

TAP

TAP

HOMEWERK

Rite a storee abowt yor day. 20 pages long.

Ha ha ha, that will keep Bill busy, thought Horrid Henry. Now, what else? What else?

Aha!

Give ten reesons why watching TV is better than reading

NEW MATHS
When does 2 + 2 =5 ?
When 2 is big enough.
Now explain why:
2+3=6
7-3=5

It was a lot more fun making up homework than doing it, thought Horrid Henry happily.

SPELLING:

Lern how to spel these words fer a test on Tuesday.

   Terrantula

   Stinkbomb

   Moosli

   Doovay

   Screem

   Intergalactik

SCEINSE

Gravity: does it work?

   Drop an egg from a hight of 30 cm onto your mum or dad's hed.

Record if it breaks. Drop another egg from a hight of 60 cm onto yor carpet. Does this egg break? Try this xperiment at least 12 times all over yor house.

Now that's what I call homework, thought Horrid Henry. He printed out the worksheets, popped them in the envelope with Miss Battle-Axe's sheet of sums, sealed it, and gave it to Dad.

'Bill's homework,' said Henry. 'Miss Battle-Axe asked me to give it to you to give to Bill's dad.'

'I'll make sure he gets it,' said Dad, putting the envelope in his briefcase. 'I'm glad to see you're becoming friends with Bill.'

Dad looked stern.

'I've got some bad news for you, Henry,' said Dad the next day.

Horrid Henry froze. What was he going to get told off about now? Oh no. Had Dad found out about what he'd done at lunchtime?

'I'm afraid Bill won't be coming back to your school,' said Dad. 'His parents have removed him. Something about new maths and a gravity experiment that went wrong.'

Horrid Henry's mouth opened. No

sound came out.

'Wha—?' gasped Horrid Henry.

'Gravity experiment?' said Mum. 'What gravity experiment?'

'Different science group,' said Henry quickly.

'Oh,' said Mum.

'Oh,' said Dad.

A lovely warm feeling spread from Henry's head all the way down to his toes.

'So Bill's not coming back?'

'No,' said Dad. 'I'm sorry that you've lost a friend.'

'I'll live,' beamed Horrid Henry.

Acknowledgements

Special thanks to Freddy Gaminara and Michael Garner for telling me so many exciting ways to cheat at football.

HORRID HENRY BOOKS

HORRiD HENRY *is also available on audio cassette and CD, all read by Miranda Richardson*

'A hoot from beginning to end . . . As always, Miranda Richardson's delivery is perfection and the manic music is a delight.' *Daily Express*

'Long may this dreadful boy continue to terrorise all who know him. He's a nightmare, but so entertaining . . . Miranda Richardson's spirited reading is accompanied by a brilliant music soundtrack – they make a noisy and fun-filled duo.' *Parents' Guide*